The Pumpkin Patch

Robin Hill School

For my mother, another McNamara

ISBN 0-439-57460-9

Text copyright © 2003 by Simon & Schuster.
Illustrations copyright © 2003 by Mike Gordon. All rights reserved.
Published by Scholastic Inc., 557 Broadway, New York, NY 10012,
by arrangement with Aladdin Paperbacks, Simon & Schuster
Children's Publishing Division. SCHOLASTIC and associated logos
are trademarks and/or registered trademarks of Scholastic Inc.

12 11 10 9 8 7 6 5 4 3 2 1   3 4 5 6 7 8/0

Printed in the U.S.A.   23

First Scholastic printing, September 2003

The text of this book was set in Century Schoolbook.

Book design by Sammy Yuen Jr.

The Pumpkin Patch

Written by Margaret McNamara
Illustrated by Mike Gordon

SCHOLASTIC INC.
New York Toronto London Auckland Sydney
Mexico City New Delhi Hong Kong Buenos Aires

"Put on your coats!"
said Mrs. Connor.

Mrs. Connor's class
was going
on a field trip
to the pumpkin patch!

Katie was ready first.
She could not wait
to find
the perfect pumpkin.

The bus ride was long.

The whole time,
Katie imagined
the perfect pumpkin.

At the pumpkin patch
there were lots and lots
of pumpkins.

"You may each
take home
one pumpkin,"
said Mrs. Connor.
"Choose carefully."

Katie began
her search.

She looked
under vines.

She looked in
the straw.

She looked
in the mud.

At last Katie found it—
the perfect pumpkin!

Mrs. Connor's class
got back on the bus.

The
Pumpkin
Patch

They showed off
their pumpkins.

"Mine is round,"
said Emma.

"Mine is tall,"
said Ayanna.

"Mine is big," said Neil.

"Look at Katie's pumpkin!"
said James.
"It is so small."

Katie's pumpkin was small.
It was very, very small.

Katie felt bad.
Her pumpkin
was not perfect.

Katie took her pumpkin home.

"I picked a bad pumpkin,"
she told her dad.

"That is not a bad pumpkin,"
he said.
"It is a good pumpkin.
Let me show you."

Katie's dad
cooked the pumpkin.
Then he cut it
into pieces.

Katie mashed the pieces.

And they made a pie.

Katie took the pie
to school.

"My pumpkin was small,"
she said.

"But it was sweet!
Now it is a pie."

The children loved
Katie's pumpkin pie.
"Your pumpkin was perfect!"
said James.